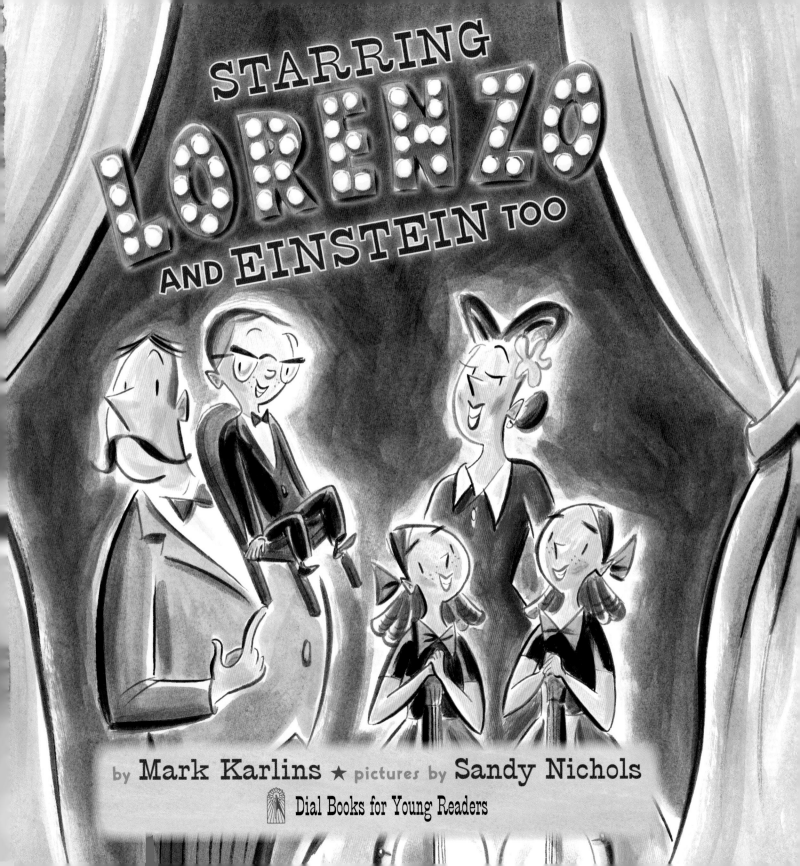

STARRING LORENZO AND EINSTEIN TOO

by **Mark Karlins** ★ pictures by **Sandy Nichols**

Dial Books for Young Readers

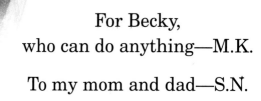

For Becky,
who can do anything—M.K.

To my mom and dad—S.N.

DIAL BOOKS FOR YOUNG READERS
A division of Penguin Young Readers Group
Published by The Penguin Group
Penguin Group (USA) Inc., 375 Hudson Street, New York, NY 10014, U.S.A.
Penguin Group (Canada), 90 Eglinton Avenue East, Suite 700, Toronto, Ontario, Canada M4P 2Y3
(a division of Pearson Penguin Canada Inc.)
Penguin Books Ltd, 80 Strand, London WC2R 0RL, England
Penguin Ireland, 25 St. Stephen's Green, Dublin 2, Ireland (a division of Penguin Books Ltd)
Penguin Group (Australia), 250 Camberwell Road, Camberwell, Victoria 3124, Australia
(a division of Pearson Australia Group Pty Ltd)
Penguin Books India Pvt Ltd, 11 Community Centre, Panchsheel Park, New Delhi - 110 017, India
Penguin Group (NZ), 67 Apollo Drive, Rosedale, North Shore 0632, New Zealand
(a division of Pearson New Zealand Ltd)
Penguin Books (South Africa) (Pty) Ltd, 24 Sturdee Avenue, Rosebank, Johannesburg 2196, South Africa
Penguin Books Ltd, Registered Offices: 80 Strand, London WC2R 0RL, England

1 3 5 7 9 10 8 6 4 2

Library of Congress Cataloging-in-Publication Data
Karlins, Mark.
Starring Lorenzo, and Einstein too / by Mark Karlins ; pictures by Sandy Nichols.
p. cm.
Summary: As a reluctant member of his family's theatrical act, The Fabulous Fortunatos,
scientifically-gifted Lorenzo is surprised to miss his family when he goes on an adventure
with the great scientist Albert Einstein.
ISBN 978-0-8037-3220-9
[1. Family life—Fiction. 2. Genius—Fiction. 3. Einstein, Albert, 1879–1955—Fiction.]
I. Nichols, Sandy, ill. II. Title.
PZ7.K14245St 2009   [E]—dc22   2008015775

Even before he was born, Lorenzo Fortunato was a very serious baby. Moving inside his mother's belly, he would close his eyes and dream that he was flying toward the moon.

In his crib, he wondered
about important matters.

Why did his rattle fall
down instead of up?

Where did the stars
go in the morning?

On the wall, he drew pictures of the planets.

His family, who performed in the theater, weren't quite sure what to make of him.

"His head's up in the clouds," his mother said.

"The boy can't even do a somersault," his father added. "I don't know what will become of him."

His twin sisters pretended
he wasn't there.

"What little brother?" asked Irene.   "I don't see a brother," said Sylvia.

As soon as he was old enough, Lorenzo joined
his parents' theater act,

THE
FABULOUS
FORTUNATOS.

Lorenzo's
father
juggled,

his mother sang,

Irene and Sylvia
played the banjo and told jokes.

His father tried to
teach him
how to
walk
on
a
tightrope.

But while he was practicing, Lorenzo wrote numbers on his
hand and nearly fell off.

None of the other things he tried worked out very well either.

The twins laughed and chanted:

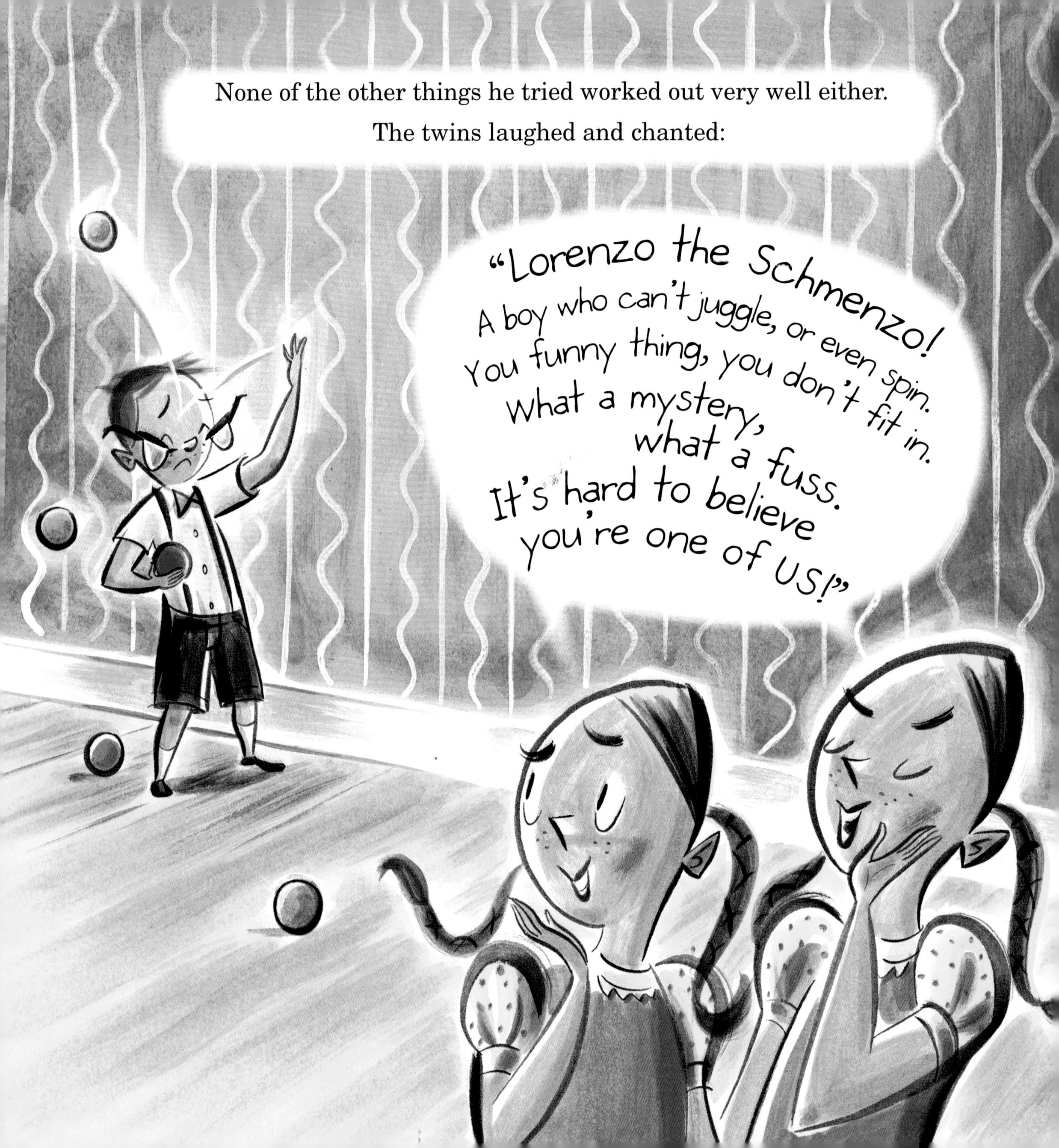
"Lorenzo the Schmenzo!
A boy who can't juggle, or even spin.
You funny thing, you don't fit in.
What a mystery,
what a fuss.
It's hard to believe
you're one of US!"

Sometimes Lorenzo felt as though he had been
born into the wrong family.

When he wasn't performing, Lorenzo lived a life more to his liking.
On the roof, inside an abandoned pigeon coop, he worked on a secret project.

He never told his family what the project was.

His family never asked.

One night, when the Fortunatos were performing, who should appear
but the great scientist Albert Einstein.

Einstein loved the Fortunatos. "After all," he said,
"who wouldn't? Such singing, such banjo playing,
such hilarious jokes!

"Not to mention the juggling skills
of Mr. Fortunato—
a lamp,
a chair,
three salamis,
and his own son,
Lorenzo,
tossed into the air!"

After the performance, Einstein went backstage to give his congratulations. Always the show-offs, the twins plucked out some fancy notes on their banjos. But Einstein only paid attention to Lorenzo.

He looked at the formula on Lorenzo's hand. He read the bottom of Lorenzo's sneaker. "Ah," he said, raising his bushy eyebrows. "Most interesting."

"You can tell what I'm working on?" Lorenzo asked.

"They don't call me a genius for nothing," Einstein replied. "Can I see it?"

Back home, Lorenzo took Einstein up to the roof.

Inside the pigeon coop was his secret project, a shiny spaceship.
"Would you like to come with me?" asked Lorenzo, and the two of
them put on space suits.

The spaceship took off with a tremendous roar. As they
traveled through the Milky Way, they scribbled formulas
on the walls of the ship and told math jokes.

Once, they even left their ship and floated freely in space.

The stars seemed to crowd close as if curious. Lorenzo wasn't sure, but he thought they were singing.

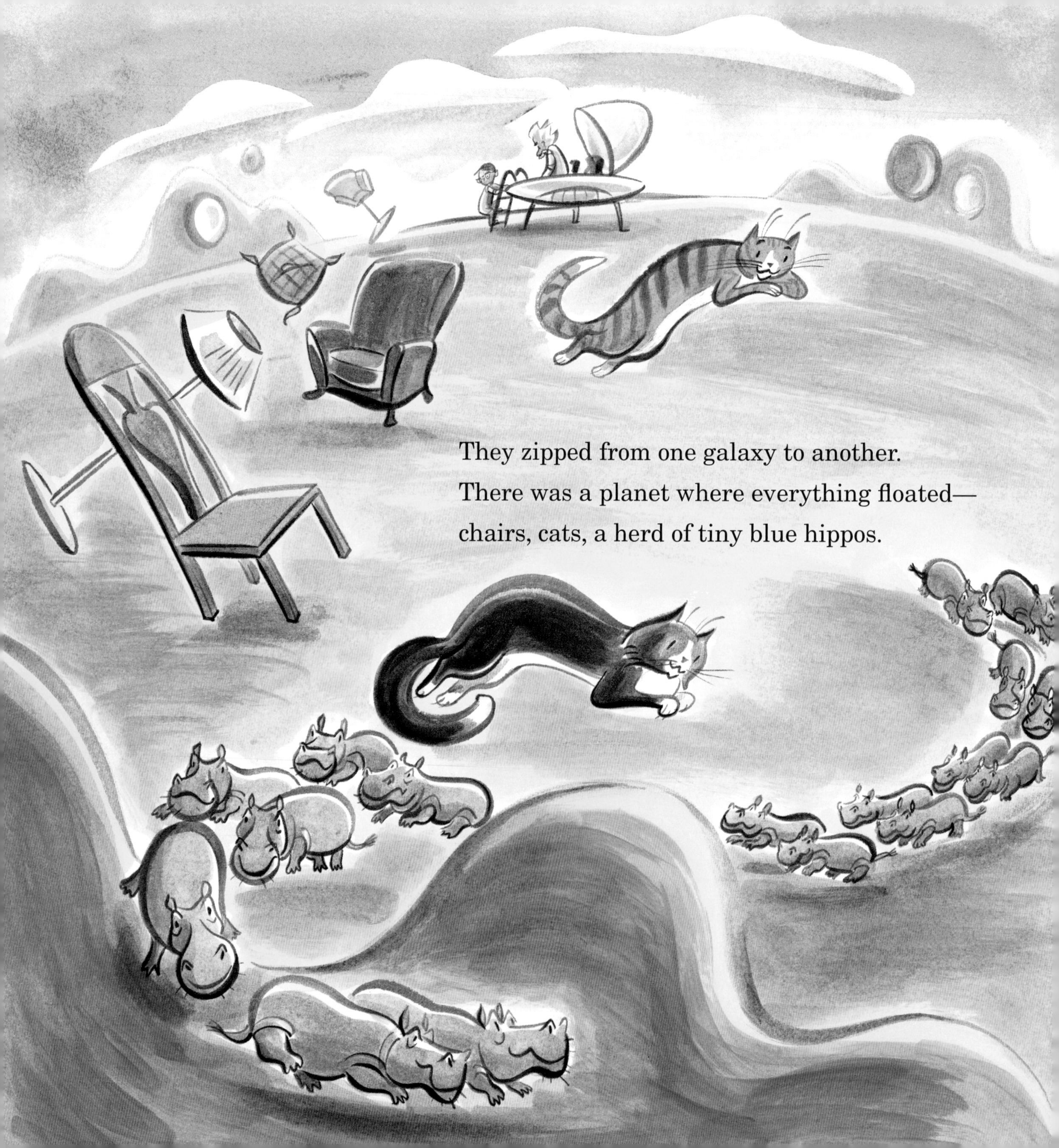

They zipped from one galaxy to another.
There was a planet where everything floated—
chairs, cats, a herd of tiny blue hippos.

On another planet everyone danced.
A deer reminded Lorenzo of his mother,
two frogs in a mud puddle of the twins.

Suddenly, Lorenzo missed his family.

When they returned to the spaceship, Lorenzo looked through the super telescope.

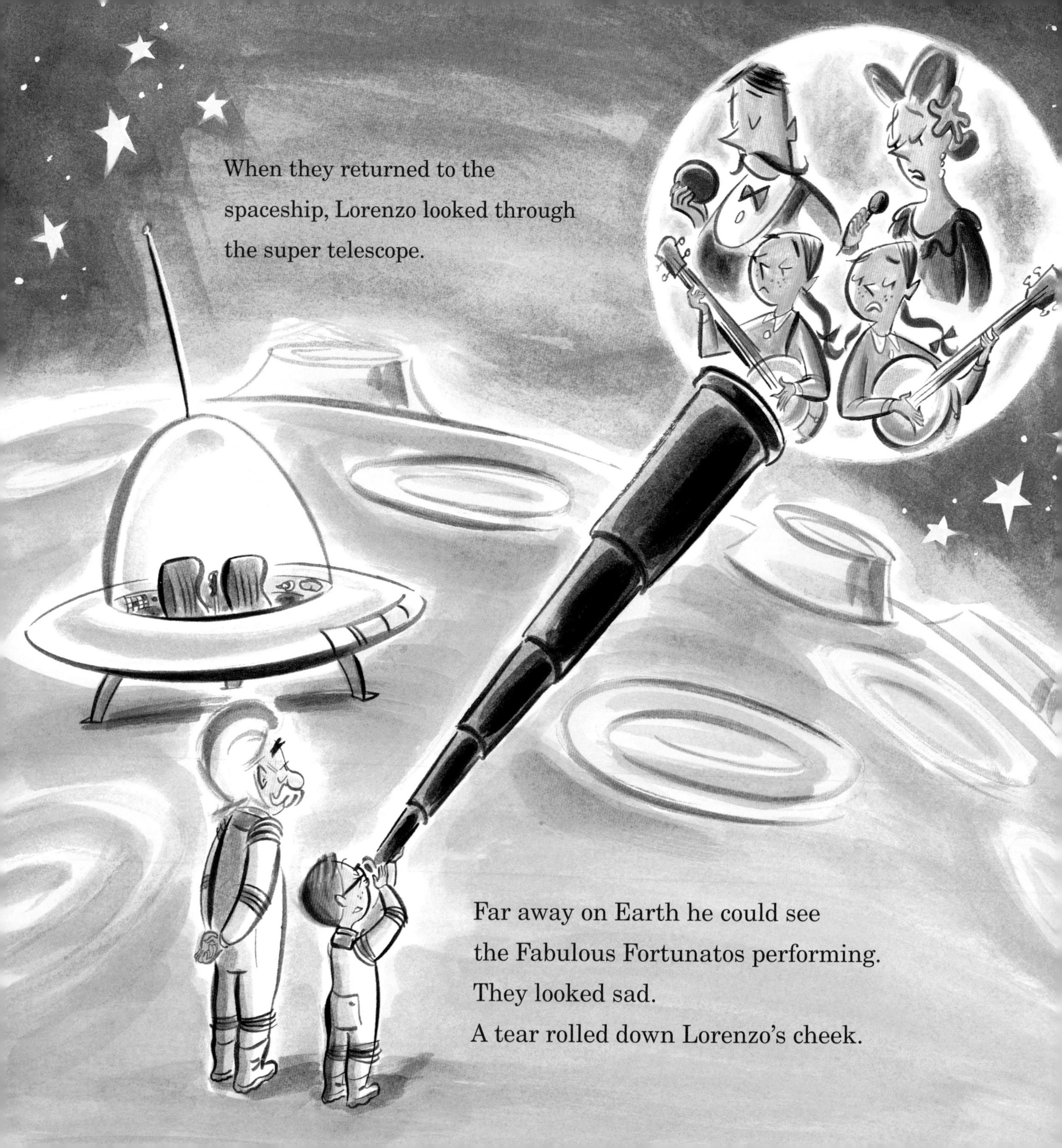

Far away on Earth he could see the Fabulous Fortunatos performing.
They looked sad.
A tear rolled down Lorenzo's cheek.

Einstein gave Lorenzo a pat on the back. "Everybody needs a family," Einstein said. "I know they miss you."

"Do you really think so?" Lorenzo gulped.

"Yes," Einstein said. "I'm sure of it."

Without another word, the two explorers put the spaceship in fast-forward and zoomed through the starry heavens.

They broke right through the roof of the theater.
Out onto the stage tumbled Lorenzo and Einstein
and a collection of creatures from outer space.

Lorenzo's family were thrilled to see him. After all the hugs and kisses, the deer, the frogs, and the floating cats began dancing with the Fortunatos.

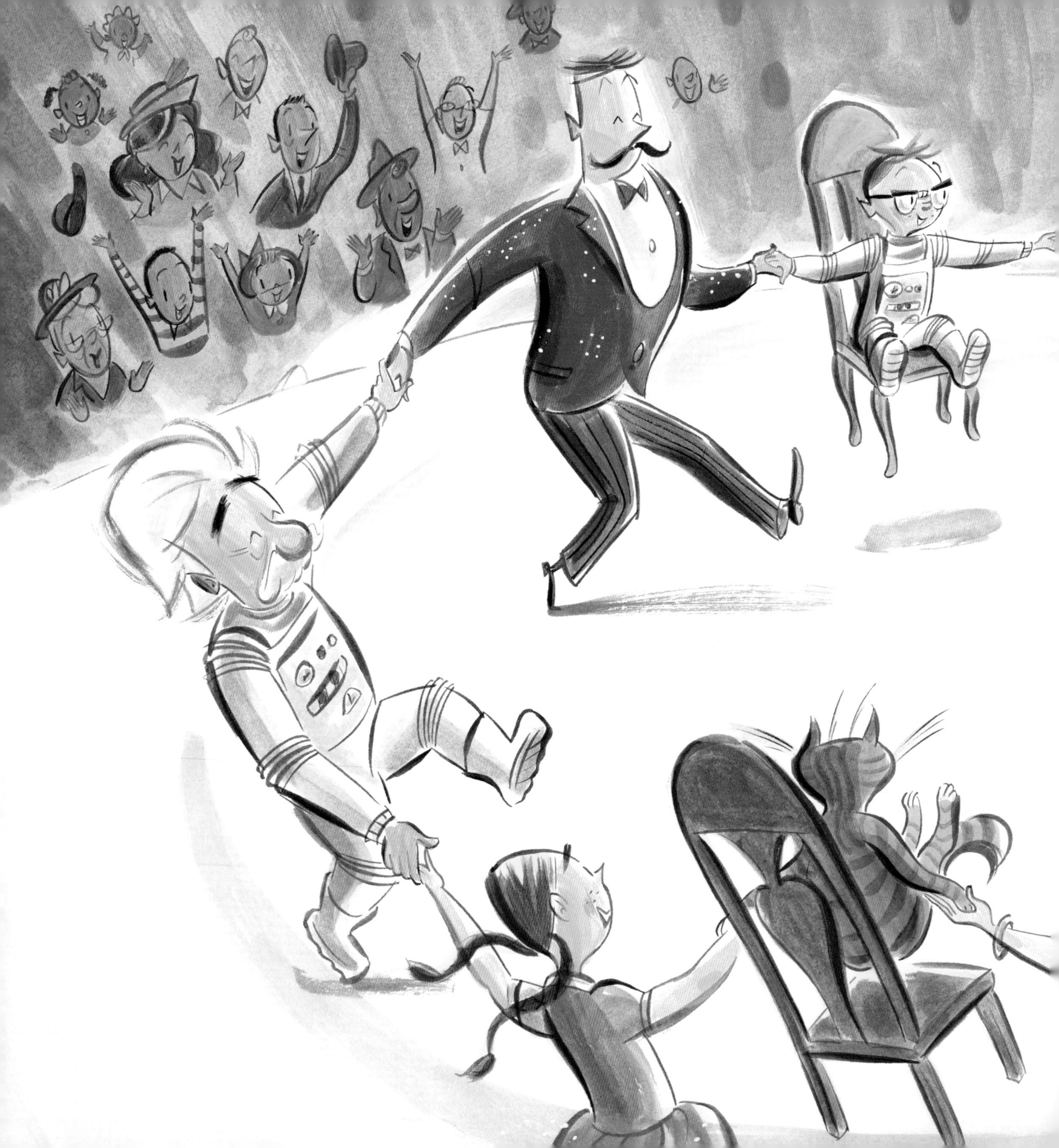

The audience cheered.
Never before had there
been such a performance!

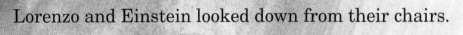

Lorenzo and Einstein looked down from their chairs.

Irene and Sylvia chanted:

"Lorenzo the Magnifico!
A boy so bright, so very clever
we thought that you were
gone forever.
A brother we
can't do without,

A FORTUNATO
THERE'S
NO DOUBT!"

"I really am a Fortunato, aren't I?" said Lorenzo.

"You are," said his mother.

"Absolutely," said his father.

Einstein just shook his wild hair and smiled.

Up above, the glittering stars moved in closer as though to watch.
And sure enough, they were singing.